Night
Gliders

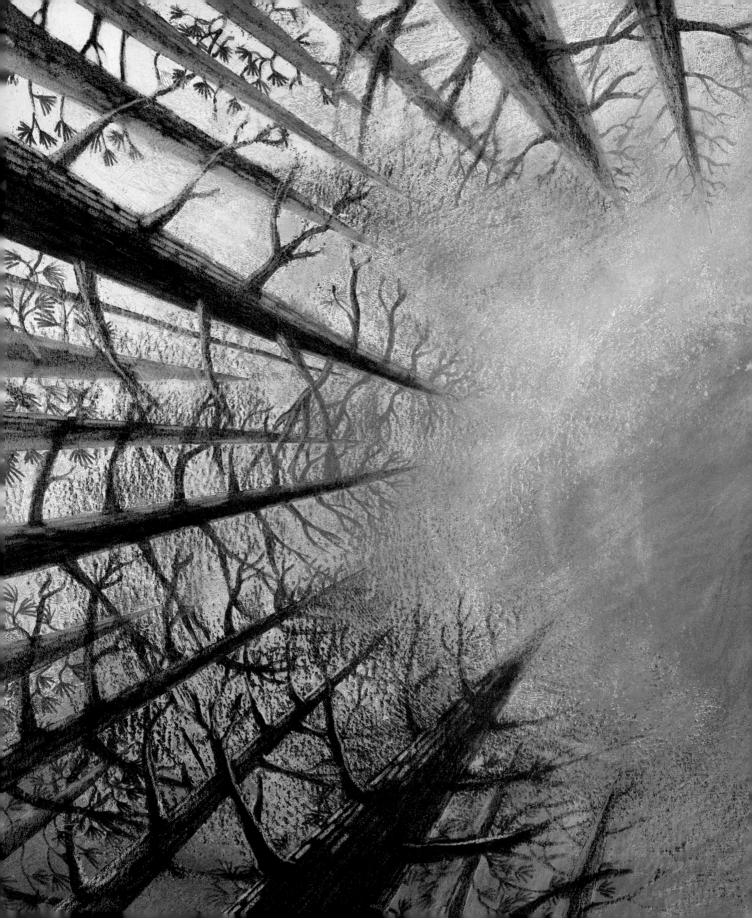

NIGHT GLIDERS

by Joanne Ryder
illustrated by Melissa Bay Mathis

BridgeWater Paperback

For Bonnie Brook
May you sail happily and far.   —J.R.

For Kyla
and in memory of Rosemary and Coriander,
gliding on together again.   —M.B.M.

Text copyright © 1996 by Joanne Ryder.

Illustrations copyright © 1996 by Melissa Bay Mathis.

Published by BridgeWater Paperback, an imprint and trademark of
Troll Communications L.L.C.

First published in hardcover by BridgeWater Books.

First paperback edition 1997.

Printed in the United States of America.

10 9 8 7 6 5 4 3 2 1

Library of Congress Cataloging-in-Publication Data

Ryder, Joanne.

Night gliders / by Joanne Ryder; pictures by Melissa Bay Mathis.

p. cm.

Summary: Four furry squirrels leap and glide though the night sky,
feeding and playing until the approach of daybreak.

ISBN 0-8167-3820-3 (lib. bdg.) ISBN 0-8167-3821-1 (pbk.)

1. Flying squirrels —Juvenile fiction. [1. Flying squirrels—Fiction.

2. Squirrels—Fiction.] I. Mathis, Melissa Bay, ill. II. Title.

PZ10.3.R954Ni   1996   [E]—dc20   95-8071

In a cozy hole
tree tall,
four furry squirrels
curl in a furry ball.

One
opens up
her eyes
and soon . . .

Eight eyes
     look out
  and watch
     the rising moon.

Four squirrels
fresh from sleep
climb up,
    look far
    and leap
        and leap.

They stretch
their furry feet
        out wide
and glide
        and glide
        and glide
                and glide.

Sailing softly,
    silently
from tree
    to tree
        to tree,
            they look below
            and watch
                their shadows
                floating
                on the moonlit snow.

Four squirrels take
    the sky path
        through the night
and find
    a little house
        with windows bright.

They leap
     from sky
toward seeds
     piled high
and gladly eat
     a nighttime treat.

They eat
     and chirp,
then dash
     from sight,
hiding nuts
     to find
some colder night.

Through the woods
the squirrels
  come
    and go
  come
    and go
leaving tiny footprints
  in the milky snow.

Four squirrels rest—
then hunt again
        and leap
            and play...
until the moon
        dips
            down
and
        down
            toward day.

And then
      and ride
          the skies
      they glide
             and sail
             back home
             with sleepy eyes.

Ahhhhh...
In their cozy hole
tree tall,
four furry squirrels
curl in a furry ball.

Author's Note

Flying squirrels are among the night's secret treasures. These common mammals often share the same forests as other squirrels in North America. But you may never realize they live overhead, because they are active only at night.

Flying squirrels cannot truly fly. But they can glide long distances from tree to tree. You may see one leap from a high branch, spreading its loose furry flaps of skin that extend from wrist to ankle. It can control its downward glide, usually landing on a lower spot on another tree. Climbing upward, it may run along tree limbs, leaping from one to another. Or it may launch itself from on high, gliding far again.

These small squirrels make nests inside protected tree cavities—often vacant woodpecker holes—or make outside tree nests of twigs and bark. They live alone or in small family groups. In winter, some join larger groups, nesting together for warmth.

Depending on the season and their woodland habitat, flying squirrels eat berries, fungi, insects, seeds, nuts, and lichen. They store food to eat when the weather is too cold, windy, or stormy for them to hunt.

If flying squirrels live nearby, they may visit your bird feeder after sunset and before sunrise. They eat sunflower seeds, peanut butter, and various nuts.

If you do see a flying squirrel gliding in the moonlight, you'll share in one of the night's special secrets.